T3-BPD-452

SHOOTING STARS

THE WOMEN OF PRO BASKETBALL

THE WOMEN OF PRO BASKETBALL

by
Bill
Gutman

Random House New York

Cover photograph credits: TOP, LEFT TO RIGHT: Allsport/Doug Pensinger; *Sports Illustrated*–Time Inc./David E. Klutho; Duomo/Chris Trotman; BOTTOM, LEFT TO RIGHT: Duomo/William Sallaz; Duomo/Darren Carroll; Duomo/Chris Trotman.

Text photograph credits: PAGE 1, TOP AND BOTTOM: Duomo/Willam Sallaz; PAGE 2, TOP AND BOTTOM: Duomo/William Sallaz; PAGE 3, TOP AND BOTTOM: Duomo/Chris Trotman; PAGE 4, TOP: Duomo/William Sallaz; PAGE 4, BOTTOM: Allsport/Marc Morrison; PAGE 5, TOP AND BOTTOM: Duomo/Chris Trotman; PAGE 6, TOP, MIDDLE, AND BOTTOM: Duomo/William Sallaz; PAGE 7, TOP AND BOTTOM: Duomo/Darren Carroll, PAGE 8, TOP: Allsport/Doug Pensinger; PAGE 8, MIDDLE: Allsport/Otto Greule; PAGE 8, BOTTOM: Duomo/William Sallaz.

 Published in the United States by Random House, Inc., New York, and simultaneously in Canada by Random House of Canada Limited, Toronto.

http://www.randomhouse.com/

Library of Congress Cataloging-in-Publication Data
Gutman, Bill.
Shooting stars: the women of pro basketball / by Bill Gutman. p. cm. SUMMARY: Traces women's participation in basketball from the early days of this sport to the recent establishment of professional women's teams and profiles some of the players who have had key roles in advancing this sport.
ISBN 0-679-89196-X (pbk.) — ISBN 0-679-99196-4 (lib. bdg.)
1. Women's National Basketball Association—History—Juvenile literature. 2. Women basketball players—United States—Juvenile literature. [1. Women basketball players. 2. Basketball—History. 3. Women's National Basketball Association.] I. Title.
GV885.515.W66G88 1998 796.323'8—dc21 97-44054

Printed in the United States of America 10 9 8 7 6 5 4 3 2 1

For Cathy

—B. G.

Contents

INTRODUCTION

"WE GOT NEXT!" For years, that short catch phrase has had a special meaning in city playgrounds around the country...or wherever pickup games of basketball are taking place. A group of two, three, or five kids walk up and announce, "We got next!" That means they're next in line to play the winners. Street talk; street rules.

But in 1997, "We got next!" came to mean something else. It was adopted as the official slogan of the newly formed Women's National Basketball Association, or WNBA. Along with the American Basketball League, or ABL (which began play several months earlier), the WNBA offered new hope that a professional basketball league for women could not only survive but also flourish.

What made people think that not only one but *two* new professional leagues for women could survive in 1997? After all, every single attempt to start a women's pro basketball league in the United States had ended in failure. The reasons for failure seemed endless: Not enough money. Not enough fans. Not enough sponsors. No televison contracts. No endorsements. Not enough marquee players.

The women's game had lagged behind the men's for years, even though the inventor of the sport intended it to be played by both men and women. By the time the National Basketball Association (NBA) began to grow and prosper in the 1960s, women were still playing a very different game. At the outset of the decade, women's college basketball still had six players to a side. Only the three forwards were allowed to score. Players could only dribble the ball three times before they had to make a pass. In a nutshell, the women's game wasn't *really* basketball.

Things finally began to change at the beginning of the 1970s. The rules were standardized.

Now the women were playing basically the same game as the men. At the same time, colleges began giving women equal scholarship opportunities. Soon, the game became more competitive, and the first women's superstars began to emerge. Players like Theresa Shank, Lusia Harris, Carol Blazejowski, Ann Meyers, and Nancy Lieberman-Cline came along to prove once and for all that women could really play. They were the game's first Shooting Stars.

Nevertheless, for the next 20 years, the collegiate court remained the ultimate stage for women basketball players in America. A few early attempts at professional leagues failed quickly. The only place American women could continue their careers was in Europe. There were a number of pro leagues in Italy, Spain, Hungary, and other countries. Eventually, women could also play for pay in such diverse places as Japan and Israel. But not in the United States, where basketball was already becoming the most popular sport among young people.

Throughout the 1980s and much of the 1990s, America's women basketball stars were playing overseas. Cynthia Cooper became fluent in Italian and Spanish. Sue Wicks spoke both those languages, and later added Japanese. They were playing the game they loved, but it wasn't an easy life. As Cooper once said, "I would score 60 points in a game, and come home to a telephone."

There was no substitute for playing in front of friends, family, and fans at home. But for the longest time, it just didn't happen. Then, in the mid-1990s, two events occurred that paved the way for women's professional basketball to take off in the United States. The first was the great interest in the Women's Final Four in 1995 and 1996. The Final Four refers to the last weekend of the post-season NCAA Tournament, when the four remaining college teams vie for the national championship. During both years the tournament sparked nearly as much interest and media coverage as the men's tourney.

Then there was the 1996 Summer Olympics in Atlanta. The United States women's basketball team not only won the gold medal, they played together for nearly a year prior to the Olympics. During that time, players like Lisa Leslie, Rebecca Lobo, Sheryl Swoopes, Ruthie

Bolton-Holifield, Dawn Staley, and Teresa Edwards became household names and sports celebrities in their own right.

So the seeds had been sown. The time was right. Then corporate America jumped on the bandwagon. And so did the very wealthy NBA. In 1996 and 1997, women's professional basketball became a reality. And this time the odds are that it's here to stay.

After just one season, many observers feel that women's professional basketball has brought some of the purity back to the game. It's a team game played mostly below the rim. It features crisp passing, tight defense, and clutch shooting—not the shoot-the-three-or-dunk game many feel the men are now playing. The women players seem to fully appreciate the opportunity that has been so long in coming. They are playing with a love of the game and an affinity for the fans that some say has been missing for too long.

The WNBA's "We got next!" may become the watchword for the next generation of basketball superstars. Only this time, they'll be on the ladies' side of the ledger. The American Basketball League has a slogan as well. It's one they hope will define part of the purpose of women's professional basketball in America: "Little girls need big girls to look up to!"

The Beginnings of the Game

Basketball is perhaps the only sport that did not evolve slowly from street games people played for fun. It was actually invented by *request.* The inventor was Dr. James Naismith, who, in 1891, was a physical education instructor at the International Young Men's Christian Association Training School in Springfield, Massachusetts. Naismith was asked to come up with an indoor game that would keep young men occupied during the cold winter months.

After giving it a great deal of thought, Naismith hung two peach baskets on the balcony of the gym, one at each end. The object of the game was to throw a soccer ball into the basket. The new game was introduced to students in December 1891. And in January 1892, Dr. Naismith wrote down the first set of 13 basic rules of the game.

The first basketball game didn't look anything like today's game. Naismith initially saw the game being played by nine men on each side. It wasn't until 1897 that five to a side became the norm for men. There was, however, something else that Naismith thought about when he invented the new sport. He felt that it could be played by women as well as men. And as early as 1892, a group of Springfield women played against a team of women teachers from the nearby Buckingham Grade School. Naismith, in fact, married one of those first women players, Maude Sherman.

The first real pioneer of women's basketball was Senda Berenson. Berenson was a student at Smith College in Northampton, Massachusetts, when she read an article by Naismith describing his new game. Berenson felt immediately that the sport might make a good game for women. But she was concerned that if the game was played by the men's rules, it might prove too strenuous. Women, as she put it, might suffer from "nervous fatigue."

So Berenson devised women's rules, which divided the court into three sections and required players to stay within their designated areas. This would later be known as the three-court game. With the three-court game, there was limited running. Players weren't allowed to sprint the length of the court.

The first women's game using the new rules was played between students at Smith College in March 1893. Berenson officiated. The participants wore dresses that buttoned up to the neck and came down below the knee. Some even played while wearing tight corsets! The clothing did not help their game, but any other kind of outfit was unthinkable at that time.

While Berenson didn't want women to lose their "grace, dignity, and self-respect while playing," she also saw basketball as important for a woman's health and well-being. One of the most common arguments in those days against paying women wages equal to that of men was that women were more likely to become ill. Berenson believed that exercise was important for this reason.

"[Women] need...all the more to develop

health and endurance if they desire to become candidates for equal wages," she said.

By 1895, basketball was being played by women in various parts of the country. The rules weren't always the same everywhere, and most of the action still took place in the Northeast. The largest criticism in those early years was that basketball simply was not a feminine activity. It wasn't ladylike to play a man's game. In the early 1900s, Agnes Wayman—a leading physical education authority of the time—had this advice for women who wanted to play basketball: "[Always have] neatly combed hair, no gum chewing or slang, never call each other by last names, and never lie or sit down on the floor."

Even Senda Berenson was concerned that if players lost their "womanliness," women would be banned from playing. She often tied games to social affairs, serving refreshments and sometimes even dinner after a game.

Despite its promising beginnings, the progress of women's basketball was painfully slow. Men's college basketball grew quickly—especially after the rules were standardized. By

1915, rules for men in colleges, YMCA's, and the Amateur Athletic Union (AAU) were all the same. Slowly, the game began to resemble what's played today.

Professional basketball—even among the men—was a different story. In the early days, no professional leagues lasted long. Teams played wherever they could. Some courts were set up in basements—with low ceilings and pillars on the court! Early pros played with a wire cage or flexible netting all around the court so the ball couldn't go out of bounds. (This is why basketball players are sometimes called "cagers.") They traveled by car, ferryboat, and train to get to games. For their efforts, they were paid between $10 and $25 per game. Most of the pros held regular jobs during the week and played only on weekends.

It wasn't until the late 1940s that professional basketball for men in the United States really took hold. That's when the Basketball Association of America merged with the National Basketball League to form the National Basketball Association. Pro hoops for men was finally here to stay.

The National Collegiate Athletic Association (NCAA) held its first post-season tournament for men in 1939. It wasn't the big thing it is today, but it was a start. By contrast, the first NCAA post-season tournament for women wasn't held until *1982,* the same year the NCAA officially began to keep women's basketball records.

Ten years earlier, however, the Association for Intercollegiate Athletics for Women (AIAW) began holding its own post-season national tournament. Even that was more than 30 years after the men. There was, however, a good reason for the delay: the rules. Up until then, the women's game was still something other than pure basketball.

Even the men's game had some archaic rules. Prior to 1938, for example, there was a center jump after every basket. That meant that after each score, players from both teams walked back to the center of the court and lined up, and the ref tossed the ball up between the two centers to start play again. This rule made continuous play impossible, eliminating the quick outlet pass and fast break after a hoop.

Since the clock kept running, the repeated center jump took precious minutes away from actual playing time. The game was slow and the scores low.

There was reason for this, however. Those who made the rules weren't sure that players had the endurance for continuous play. They didn't think most men could run up and down the court nonstop for 40 minutes a game. And if the lords of basketball at the time didn't feel men could run for a whole game, they certainly didn't think women could, either. This is probably the major reason women's rules took so long to change.

Women didn't need a center jump because they had the three-court game, where players had to stay within an assigned area. No player was allowed to run the full court. In 1938, the same year the center jump was eliminated for men, the women's game changed from the three-court game to the two-court game. There were now six players to a side, three forwards and three guards. Only the forwards could score. But women were still allowed only one dribble before a pass and couldn't run the full court.

By this time, basketball had become an Olympic sport for men, having been introduced at the 1936 Games in Berlin, Germany. It would take another 40 years for women's basketball to become a medal sport at the Olympics.

Then, in 1949–50, the women's game finally allowed a player two dribbles before she was forced to pass. That rule lasted until 1961–62, when three bounces or dribbles were permitted. A year later, two of the six players were allowed to leave their "zones" and rove the entire court. And, finally, in 1966–67, women were allowed unlimited dribbling. But it still took until the 1971–72 season for women's basketball at the collegiate level to adopt a five-player, full-court game with a 30-second shot clock. Finally, women were playing real basketball at last.

That same year there was another event that helped the women's game take a giant step. President Richard Nixon signed Title IX of the Educational Amendment of 1972. This amendment provided more money for women's athletic programs, allowing for athletic scholarships, uniforms, full-time coaches, and major schedules. This important piece of federal legislation would be the final piece to the puzzle. It would bring women's basketball at the college level into the 20th century. Unfortunately, nearly three-quarters of a century had passed before it happened. But to use an old cliché, better late than never.

2 THE STARS BEGIN TO SHINE

Until the rules were finally modernized and Title IX was signed, it was nearly impossible for women to become big-name basketball stars. There were a couple of early attempts, now nearly entirely forgotten. For instance, in 1926 the AAU sponsored a national women's basketball championship. They allowed the women to use the men's rules at the time. But nothing really came of it.

And then there were the Red Heads. In 1936, a group of talented, athletic women formed a basketball team to barnstorm and play exhibition games. They played by men's rules and against men's teams. The gimmick was that these women were required to wear makeup, look beautiful, and play well. And they had to either wear red wigs or dye their hair red!

Sure, it was a promotional hook to make money. But the Red Heads could really play the game, and they more than held their own against various men's teams. The team didn't stay around very long, however, and the players are now largely forgotten.

Of all the early women stars, the best had to be Nera White. Born in 1935, White attended George Peabody College in Nashville from 1954–58, where she played under the restrictive rules of the time. But after graduation, White spent 15 years leading a team sponsored by the Nashville Business College to ten AAU national championships. She was named the tournament's Most Valuable Player all ten times! She was also on various all-star teams that traveled the world, playing in numerous foreign countries.

Though she was a player before her time, Nera White's achievements were recognized in 1992 when she was elected to the Basketball Hall of Fame. During the enshrinement ceremonies, films of White in action mesmerized everyone.

"How in the world could a 6'1" slender woman handle the ball like [Bob] Cousy, take jump shots like Jerry West, and go to the basket like Oscar Robertson?" said Ann Meyers, herself a superstar of the women's game. "[White] was incredible. [Even the] men were awestruck at her ability."

Though Nera White was a singular exception, it wasn't until after 1972 that the face of women's basketball changed forever. Women who worked hard to develop their basketball skills now had a stage on which to perform. As soon as the rules changed and the AIAW began to hold its national championship tourney, a superteam emerged. Immaculata College in Immaculata, Pennsylvania, won the first three tournaments. The Mighty Macs defeated West Chester University, Queens College, and Mississippi College in the finals in 1972, 1973, and 1974 to become three-time champs.

During that time, Coach Cathy Rush and her team compiled a 64–2 record. They were led by a 5'11" center named Theresa Shank, perhaps the first superstar in the women's collegiate game. The schools involved in those three title games—Immaculata, West Chester, Queens College, and Mississippi College—were fairly small. The big, traditional schools had not yet gotten their programs in gear. But that was coming quickly.

Another milestone in women's basketball came in February 1975. One night, some 12,000 fans paid their way into Madison Square Garden in New York City. They were there to watch a regular-season game between defending champ Immaculata College and Queens College. For that many fans to come to an arena known as the Basketball Capital of the World was a real indication that the women's game was here to stay.

In fact, the entire evening was introduced by the playing of the song "I Am Woman" by Helen Reddy. The song reflected the pride of all women. But these women had more than pride. They had skills and court savvy, and could shoot the basketball. In short, they gave the fans their money's worth.

During the next few years, a whole new group of college superstars would emerge, players still remembered as great pioneers of the women's game. They were the ones who paved the way for everything that followed, including the eventual creation of the WNBA and the ABL. Let's take a quick look at a few of these outstanding Shooting Stars.

Lusia Harris

Lusia Harris followed Theresa Shank as the most dominant player in the women's ranks. She played four years at Delta State University in Cleveland, Mississippi. During that time, the 6'3" center led her team to an amazing 109–6 record and three AIAW national championships from 1975–77. In her four years, she scored 2,981 points (a 25.9 average) and grabbed 1,662 rebounds (a 14.5 average).

Harris was so good that she became the first woman ever drafted by an NBA team. The New Orleans (now Utah) Jazz drafted her in 1977, but she decided against going to training camp.

"I figured there was no sense in it," she said. "I am 6'3". No way could I compete against the men at my position. When they [drafted] me, I was honored. But I thought it was probably just a publicity thing."

A member of the first United States women's basketball Olympic team, Harris helped her country win a silver medal at the 1976 Olympics. Now Lusia Harris-Stewart, she is a mother of four and a health and physical education teacher in her home state of Mississippi. She is also a coach of a girls' high school team. She was elected to the Basketball Hall of Fame in 1992.

Carol Blazejowski

"The Blaze" may still be the best pure scorer ever to play in the women's collegiate ranks. She was a three-time All-American at Montclair State in New Jersey, and continues to hold the NCAA career scoring mark for women—31.7 points a game. She also holds the single-season mark, averaging an incredible 38.6 points a game in 1977–78. That year, she became the first woman to receive the Wade Trophy as Women's Basketball Player of the Year.

On the night of March 6, 1977, the Blaze

electrified a crowd of 12,000 fans at Madison Square Garden by scoring 52 points in a game against Queens College. Since that time, no collegiate player, male or female, has scored more points in a single game at the Garden.

Blazejowski grew up playing in pickup games with boys. At first they didn't want to let her play. But before long, she was always the first pick. And much of her early encouragement came from her family.

"My parents believed that as long as I was safe and wasn't hurting anyone, then playing sports seemed natural," she said. "There were never any restrictions."

After her college career ended, the 5'10" Blaze became a member of the 1979 Pan American Games team and was selected to the 1980 Olympic team (though the United States boycotted those Games, held in Moscow). She then played for the New Jersey Gems in the Women's Basketball League (WBL) in 1980–81. She was the leading scorer in that early women's pro league, but never even received her full salary because the league went bankrupt.

After working for the NBA for six years, the Blaze became vice president and general manager of the New York Liberty of the WNBA in 1997. She still plays basketball on weekends, often against bigger, stronger men. Yet, as always, she holds her own. Frank Martinuk, a former University of Vermont player who has played with and against Blazejowski for 11 years, still marvels at her talent.

"As far as shooting ability, there is probably no one better," said Martinuk. "Technically, she can't be matched. But what she does best is her fundamentals, getting the shot off, moving without the ball. She really understands how to play basketball. Occasionally, some other women come down to play, but it's really not fair for her to play against them. She'd destroy them. They don't have a chance."

Forty years old when the WNBA started in 1997, Blazejowski was asked several times if she wanted to put on a uniform and play in the new league. But she said no.

"I made my mark in history as a player," she explained. "Now I can make my mark as an executive. My life is basketball, and now I can give back to the game, give back to its growth. I am passionate about this sport, about this league, about this team. I want to do it right."

That's Carol Blazejowski, a great player, a Hall of Famer in every sense of the word.

Ann Meyers

Ann Meyers was a good-enough basketball player to try out for the Indiana Pacers of the NBA. And why not? Just listen to some of her basketball accomplishments. She was the first high school player to make a United States national team. She was the first woman to receive a full athletic scholarship to UCLA, as well as the first woman player named to Kodak's All-American team four straight seasons. She also played on the first women's Olympic basketball team in 1976 and was the first woman player drafted by the WBL when it was formed in 1978.

That's a lot of "firsts." Then in September 1979, the Indiana Pacers signed the 24-year-old Meyers to a $50,000 contract and invited her to a rookie, free-agent training camp. Though many people thought the Pacers were just looking for publicity, Meyers didn't back down. She went to the camp and gave it her all. And in doing so, she gave women's basketball still another shot in the arm.

Meyers didn't back down from the bigger, stronger players, even taking a hard charge from veteran John Kuester.

"Everyone's going for a job," Kuester said at the time. "She understands that. I bumped her down low. She's used to contact. My first impression was she wants to play."

Though Meyers was cut after three days, she felt she had more than held her own. "I'm not saying I was as quick or as fast as some of those guys," she explained, "but I thought I had performed well enough to make it past the tryouts like some of the other free agents and rookies."

Pacers coach Bob Leonard, who had been against the tryout, came away with newfound respect for Meyers.

"If she were six inches taller and 40 pounds heavier, it would have been a different story," Leonard said. "I personally feel Ann did a great job from a fundamental standpoint of knowing the game of basketball. I wish some guys out there were as fundamentally sound as her."

Not surprisingly, Ann Meyers is now in the Basketball Hall of Fame. Her late husband, Don Drysdale, is a member of the Baseball Hall of Fame, making them the first husband-and-wife team to both be elected to a sports Hall of Fame. Today she is a sports commentator who still looks back on her tryout with the Pacers as perhaps her most cherished memory.

"I did it because I didn't want to look back and wonder, 'What if?'" Meyers said. "My main purpose was to go in as a ballplayer, to hold my head up and do my best."

That Ann Meyers *always* did.

Nancy Lieberman-Cline

Nancy Lieberman-Cline is a pioneer player who just keeps rolling along. At the age of 38, she decided to play for the Phoenix Mercury in the inaugural 1997 season of the WNBA, her final stop in a career that has already seen her inducted into the Basketball Hall of Fame. It all started for the 5'10" native of Brooklyn, New

York, on the blacktop playground courts of the city. She learned the fundamentals of the game early and in 1976 was a member of the silver medal–winning United States Olympic team. Lieberman-Cline was just 17 years old then, making her the youngest player in history to win an Olympic basketball medal.

But that was only the beginning. From there, Lieberman-Cline became a three-time All-American at Old Dominion University, leading her team to a 72–2 record and a pair of national championships in 1979 and 1980. As a collegian, she scored 2,430 points, had 1,167 rebounds, and handed out 961 assists. She won the Wade Trophy as Player of the Year on two occasions.

Like most top women players then, Nancy Lieberman-Cline hoped to play professionally. She became the top draft choice of the WBL's Dallas Diamonds in 1980, leading the team in scoring and then into the championship series in the 1981 playoffs. But the WBL folded after the season, and Lieberman-Cline was forced to look for new basketball worlds to conquer.

With no professional women's league in existence, Lieberman-Cline took on another challenge. She became the first woman to play in a men's professional league. In 1986, she was a member of the Springfield Fame of the now-defunct United States Basketball League. A year later, she played for the Long Island Knights of the USBL, more than holding her own. She was also a member of the Washington Generals, the team that travels with and plays against the Harlem Globetrotters (a team of skilled players who entertain fans with their comedy routines and basketball wizardry).

After a short time with the Generals (where she met and married her husband, Tim Cline), Lieberman-Cline moved on to other ventures. She became a broadcaster, started her own sports marketing firm, and wrote columns about the game for several publications. But when the WNBA came along, Lieberman-Cline made a decision. Unlike many of the stars from her era, she decided to play again.

"I wanted to show myself that I can still play the game at this level," Lieberman-Cline said. "At some point if it's not fun, I'll stop. There's no reason for me to play; I have nothing to prove. I *want* to do this."

Like the other superstars of the women's game, Nancy Lieberman-Cline has always been able to back up her words with deeds.

Lynette Woodard

Lynette Woodard is another great star of the women's game who showed her moxie when there wasn't a league to call her own. She became the first woman to play with the Harlem Globetrotters. And she came to the Trotters with first-class credentials. In four years at the University of Kansas, Woodard became the top scorer in women's history, with 3,649 points. She was a four-time All-American and the winner of the Wade Trophy in 1981. Along the way she averaged 26.3 points a game and shot 52.5 percent from the field.

A 6'0" guard, Woodard played an exceptional all-around game. Like the other superstars of her time, she was a fundamentally sound player. She was a member of the United States Olympic team in 1980 and the gold medal–winning team of 1984. But where to from there?

In 1985, Lynette became a member of the

Globetrotters. Her cousin, Hubert "Geese" Ausbie, had been the Trotters' lead player for 24 years and later their coach. Woodard entertained fans with her dazzling passes, her ability to twirl basketballs on her fingertips, and her amazing shooting skills.

After two years with the Trotters, she played pro in Italy through 1989, then moved her skills to Japan until 1993. Finally, she retired and became a registered stockbroker for Magna Securities in New York City. Then, at age 37—not having played competitively for five years—Woodard decided to return to the court and play for the Cleveland Rockers of the WNBA.

"I wished and hoped for a league like this for so long," she said. "It's a special thing to be able to do one of the things that you love most in life. When I was very young, I used to play for awards and trophies. I loved them. But this is what I want to do today. I just love to play the game."

Cheryl Miller

Reggie Miller is the star shooting guard for the Indiana Pacers, an NBA All-Star, and one of the great streak shooters in the history of the game. Yet there are those who still tell Reggie he's the second-best player in the Miller family. That's because his sister Cheryl is arguably the best women's basketball player ever.

Miller followed Ann Meyers and Lynette Woodard as the third player ever to be named to the Kodak All-American team for four straight years. She was also a three-time winner of the Naismith Award as the best women's college player in the land. At 6'3", Miller was the first woman to blend the power and height of a post player with the speed and passing skills of a guard. In a word, she could do it all.

Miller led the Lady Trojans of the University of Southern California to a pair of national championships in 1983 and 1984, and she helped the United States to Olympic gold in 1984. She was elected to the Basketball Hall of Fame in 1995. Like most of the great stars, she didn't want to leave the game, even though there wasn't a professional league for women in America.

So Miller returned to USC as a coach for two years, winning the 1994 Pac-10 title and taking her teams to a pair of NCAA tournaments. After that, she became a broadcaster, the first woman to work NBA games as an analyst and commentator. When the WNBA formed, many thought the 33-year-old Miller would come out of retirement and play once more. She would, everyone felt, become one of the league's top stars.

But with a history of knee problems and a great career already behind her, Miller opted instead to become the coach and general manager of the Phoenix Mercury.

"I have no desire to play," she said. "I've had no desire to play since I last walked off the floor. I think I'm one of the luckiest human beings on this planet to be able to have walked away from something knowing that I accomplished everything I wanted to...I've been blessed in everything that I do. I've got a great broadcasting career and I coached a little bit at USC, and now I get the opportunity to do both."

As for her brother, Reggie Miller regrets

that his big sister is not playing once more.

"Cheryl could dunk," he said, "she could pass like Magic [Johnson], and she could shoot like Larry [Bird]. No question. No woman would have been able to stop her.

"Any time you have one woman who has meant so much to the game, hey, that's why so many young women look up to her."

Nera White, Lusia Harris, Carol Blazejowski, Ann Meyers, Nancy Lieberman-Cline, Lynette Woodard, and Cheryl Miller. These are some of the biggest stars and pioneers who brought the women's game into the modern age. There were other great players from their generation as well, some of whom continue to play, some who don't. But all have an innate love of the game and have remained connected to it in one way or another.

Though all of these great players may not reap the rewards of professional basketball for women, they were the pioneers who paved the way. They brought women's basketball into the modern age with their skill, determination, and drive. Those playing today owe these stars a debt of gratitude and don't have to look far to tell them. They're all still legends, and still around.

3 Sowing the Seeds

Despite the fact that many great women basketball players emerged in the 1970s, 1980s, and early 1990s, there was one huge, unavoidable chasm that none of them could surmount. There was no main stage, no place in America where a top-flight woman basketball star could play the game she loved and be paid for doing it.

It was a completely different story with the men. The NBA grew by leaps and bounds in the 1980s, especially after Magic Johnson, Larry Bird, and then Michael Jordan joined the league. Basketball was enjoying an unprecedented popularity. It was quickly becoming *the* sport around the world. The pros in America were earning millions of dollars per year and were becoming full-fledged national celebrities.

Why wasn't there a woman's league?

It wasn't that a pro league for women had not been tried. There had been a number of attempts. Some were so brief, so ludicrous, that there is debate over how many leagues sprang up and died over the years. Some say three; some say five. Others say seven. But no one will argue about the number that succeeded. That's unanimous. None.

There was the Women's Professional Basketball League (WBL), which debuted on December 9, 1978. It was an eight-team league that signed many of the top collegiate players. But the time wasn't right. Even the NBA hadn't really hit its boom period in 1978, and the WBL limped along for three seasons before going bankrupt.

By 1991, the times were better. That's when someone had the bright idea of starting the Liberty Basketball Association for women. The people behind the league, however, had some strange ideas about women's basketball. They decided to create a game with shorter courts and lower hoops, and to have the players wear tight-fitting spandex uniforms. This wasn't what women wanted, but with no place else to play, many decided to sign up. The joke was on everyone. The Liberty Basketball Association folded after only a single exhibition game.

A year later, there was yet another attempt. This one was called the Women's World Basketball Association (WWBA). It was situated in the Midwest with six teams and was a legitimate attempt to finally get a women's pro league to stick. But the money wasn't there, and after a total of three seasons, the WWBA was no more.

By now it was 1995, and basketball was a major sport all around the world. The NBA had sent its first "Dream Team" of NBA stars to the 1992 Olympics in Barcelona, Spain. There, the likes of Magic Johnson, Michael Jordan, Larry Bird, Charles Barkley, Karl Malone, David Robinson, Scottie Pippen, and Clyde Drexler helped spread the popularity of the sport even more. They also won gold going away. The United States women's team that year won a bronze medal.

Many of the top women players continued to toil in leagues in Europe and Asia. It was still basketball, and it was an education for them.

But it wasn't playing before the home fans.

But just as the WWBA became the latest failed attempt at a women's pro league, two events were about to occur that would push the women's game into the 21st century. These events would send a message to corporate America as well as to the nation's sports fans. The message was that it was no longer necessary to make the best women basketball players in America leave the country in order to play as professionals, that women's professional basketball could be a great game and wonderful entertainment for the entire family.

The first event was the heightened interest generated by the post-season NCAA national championship tournament for women. The men's Final Four had been a major event for years, but as with every other development in basketball, the women's tournament lagged behind in interest and coverage. Then the women's Final Four got a real shot in the arm in 1993, when Texas Tech senior Sheryl Swoopes scored a record 47 points as her team beat Ohio State, 84–82, for the title. It was the most points anyone—male or female—had ever scored in an NCAA championship game.

Despite her great success, Swoopes was playing basketball in Italy a year later. That was what had to change.

It wasn't until 1995 that the women's Final Four caught the fancy of the sports-loving public as a whole. Television hype helped. And so did the University of Connecticut Lady Huskies, who began to write a story of their own in the 1994–95 season.

Led by a 6'4" center/forward named Rebecca Lobo, the Lady Huskies ripped through the regular season with an unblemished record. During their unbeaten run, the team began receiving as much publicity and media coverage as any women's team ever had. At the same time, Rebecca Lobo began getting the kind of superstar coverage that was usually reserved for the men.

People learned that the senior star was from Southwick, Massachusetts, and had been a four-year starter and star for the Lady Huskies. Lobo was also an Academic All-American, a candidate for a prestigious Rhodes Scholarship, and a

1994 Kodak All-American. They also found out that while Lobo continued to work toward a degree in political science *and* lead her unbeaten basketball team, she was involved in another battle back home.

Her mother, RuthAnn Lobo, had been diagnosed with breast cancer when Rebecca was a junior. In spite of everything on her plate, Rebecca Lobo was a source of strength for her mother as she underwent treatment for the disease. The two would later co-write a mother-daughter autobiography, *The Home Team,* which would chronicle their relationship and RuthAnn's battle against breast cancer. It would be published in 1996.

By Final Four time, the Lady Huskies were still unbeaten and in line for the national championship. The championship game pitted Connecticut against another outstanding team, the Lady Vols from the University of Tennessee. It turned out to be a great game, with the Lady Vols leading 38–32 at halftime. But Lobo and her teammates would not be denied. They came on strong during the final minutes, taking the lead with less than two minutes remaining in the game. The final score was 70–64, with UConn winning its first national championship.

Once again the star was Rebecca Lobo. She led all scorers with 17 points and was named the tournament's Outstanding Player.

"We didn't have the best basketball players or the best basketball team in the country," Lobo would say later. "We just had a team that worked incredibly well together."

The Lady Huskies finished the season with a spotless 35–0 record—the most victories in a season by any NCAA basketball team, men's or women's. And the victory was just the beginning for Rebecca Lobo.

She received a slew of post-season honors, including the Wade Trophy as Player of the Year. That was followed by an appearance on *The Late Show with David Letterman* and a jog with President Bill Clinton during a visit to the White House. She took it all in with grace and dignity.

Less than a year later, the Spalding company would introduce the Rebecca Lobo basketball to the buying public. Corporate America was waking up.

“Rebecca is a phenomenon,” said Anne Flannery, the director of women’s athletics at Spalding. “Cheryl Miller had her day. She took women’s basketball to another level. Then Sheryl Swoopes took it one step farther. But no one else had had the combination of dynamics that Rebecca and the UConn team enjoyed.”

Those “dynamics” included more press coverage than any other team in the history of women’s basketball. The timing didn’t hurt, either. There was a growing discontent with some of the elements of men’s sports, and an increasing interest in women’s sports in general. It also didn’t hurt that the University of Connecticut was located close to all-sports television station ESPN and to New York City, still considered the media center of the country.

In the two years following UConn’s dramatic success, there was more attention paid to women’s college basketball than ever before. Tennessee, which was runner-up to UConn in 1995, would win the national championship the next two years. In the 1996 semi-final, the Lady Vols defeated defending champion UConn in a great overtime game, 88–83, then topped Georgia, 83–65, for the title. The championship game at the Charlotte Coliseum was witnessed by 23,291 fans, the largest crowd ever to watch an NCAA women's final.

The Lady Vols were led by a talented freshman, Chamique Holdsclaw, who scored 16 points and grabbed 14 rebounds in the final. But perhaps it was senior point guard Michelle Marciniak (the tournament's Most Outstanding Player) who best expressed how far the women's game had come.

She said that when she was growing up playing basketball, she didn't pretend to be Larry Bird or Michael Jordan. Rather, she pretended to be herself, winning a national title for her college team.

"Ever since I was a little girl I had a dream of cutting down the nets, being out on the floor with a national championship team," she said. "I can't believe it's come true."

A year later, the Vols did it again. Their final victory over Old Dominion, 68–59, gave the team and its coach, Pat Summitt, their fifth NCAA title. Once again the media coverage was immense. Summitt became a big story. She had now coached more national championship teams than any other coach in NCAA history except for UCLA's legendary John Wooden. Wooden led the men's Bruin team to ten NCAA championships. Now a woman was in second place as a title-winning coach.

Once again, Chamique Holdsclaw was the star. She scored 24 points in the final game and was the Outstanding Player in the Final Four. By the end of her sophomore year, she was already a two-time All-American. A product of the New York City playgrounds, she was part of the new breed of women stars, playing basketball nearly all her life. Nancy Lieberman-Cline, who was doing TV commentary on the Final Four, was impressed.

"I think Cheryl [Miller] is the best ever, but before all is said and done, Chamique could be better."

So a whole new lineage of players was beginning to form. Lieberman-Cline, a superstar from an earlier generation, was comparing great players from the generations that followed her. And by the time Tennessee won its fifth title in April 1997, there were already two new women's professional leagues in existence.

The women playing in the new leagues—as well as the collegians like Holdsclaw who looked forward to playing as a pro someday—had observed many of the things that had happened to men's professional sports. They had seen more and more collegians leave school before their senior years to play for pay. The NBA was even beginning to draft high school seniors before they went to college. Holdsclaw, a political science major at Tennessee, spoke for many when she voiced her feelings on how it should be.

"I don't think females should be allowed to decide to go pro," she said. "The leagues need mature young ladies who have their degrees."

Just a few years earlier, these kinds of opinions would have gone unnoticed. But now the stars of the women's game were being heard. They were being sought out for interviews with the same fervor that followed the men's game. And their opinions appeared in newspapers, on radio and television, and in major magazines all over the country.

So the emergence of the women's NCAA Tournament and the Final Four had a major effect on the demand to see more women's basketball. The intense media coverage of the tourney convinced those who wanted to start a professional league for women that this time it would work. And even after the new pro leagues were formed, the collegiate game continued to grow and flourish.

But there was another major event that helped lead to the formation of the WNBA and the ABL. That was the high-profile women's Dream Team, a team chosen and groomed to win the gold at the 1996 Olympic Games in Atlanta. It would be a team that was prepared and showcased in a way never before seen in the United States.

An Olympic Dream and Much More

By the mid-1990s, basketball was no longer just an American sport. The court game for both men and women was growing and thriving in many countries. United States all-star or international teams did not always win automatically. In the Olympics, the United States women won gold medals in 1984 and 1988. But in 1992, the U.S. team finished a disappointing third.

In the past, the American Olympic team was chosen just a few weeks before the start of the Summer Games. But Olympic officials felt this was just not enough time for a group of diverse individual players to mesh into a smooth working team. With the 1996 Summer Games still more than a year away, the officials decided to do things a bit differently.

They decided to select a women's national team in May 1995. The team would then embark on a nine-month tour, playing both at home and abroad. They would compete against international teams, foreign national teams, and some of the best collegiate teams in America. The head coach was Tara VanDerveer, who had taken a leave of absence from her coaching position at Stanford University to guide the Olympians.

"By playing together for an extended period of time," VanDerveer said, "the players on the national team can learn each other's idiosyncrasies. That is what this year is for—learning the nuances of the game. It's not X's and O's, ball handling, and shooting. It's anticipating what a teammate will do."

During those nine months, the team would travel more than 100,000 miles all over the world. Besides getting ready to compete in the Games themselves, the players also became ambassadors for top-flight women's basketball. They found themselves to be high-profile celebrities who began attracting more and more attention. And they proved, once and for all, that women basketball players were not only great athletes but also a marketable commodity. People wanted to see them play. Corporate sponsors wanted them to endorse products. They were quickly becoming role models for a new generation.

The team was a mixture of veteran players with previous Olympic and international experience and younger players who had recently exited the college ranks. The core of the 1996 women's Olympic basketball team consisted of 11 outstanding players.

Teresa Edwards, a veteran of three previous Olympic teams (1984, 1988, 1992), was the most experienced. She was a high-scoring guard who had been an All-American at Georgia back in 1985 and 1986. Katrina McClain followed Edwards at Georgia and was the Women's Basketball Coaches Association Player of the Year in 1987. Both Edwards and McClain were past their 30th birthday and had been playing overseas for years.

They were joined by Ruthie Bolton-Holifield, who graduated from Auburn in 1989 after helping her team to a four-year record of 119–13;

Jennifer Azzi of Stanford, who won the Wade Trophy in 1990; and Dawn Staley of Virginia, who was the 1991 Wade Trophy recipient. Carla McGhee, a 6'2" center/forward who graduated from Tennessee in 1990, and Katy Steding, who had played for Coach VanDerveer at Stanford, were also on the team. One of the younger players was guard Nikki McCray of Tennessee, who had just graduated in 1995.

Then there were the three players who would be the focus of much of the media attention. Lisa Leslie was a 6'5" center who had been an All-American at USC in 1993 and 1994. Not only was she an outstanding scorer, rebounder, and shot-blocker, but she was also a tall, elegant woman who had modeled professionally. She was a natural for the media spotlight.

Sheryl Swoopes, who had scored 47 points in the NCAA title game in 1993, was an outstanding 6'0" forward who had the distinction of being the first woman player in history to have a shoe named after her. In the fall of 1995, Nike came out with the "Air Swoopes" basketball shoe.

The final member of the team was Rebecca

Lobo. Because of her name recognition and recent success with the UConn team, she was often the early focus of media attention. But Lobo was always quick to try deflecting the spotlight elsewhere.

"Some people who've only been fans for the past couple of years may know my name or Sheryl's," she said. "But as they watch our team play, they'll get to know us all. And then they'll recognize that Teresa and Katrina are phenomenal basketball players."

Playing for the national team wasn't an easy decision for some of the players. Because team members would have to devote a full year to their effort, they would be paid $50,000 by USA Basketball. But for the seasoned pros who were already stars in Europe, that could mean a very sizable reduction in income.

For instance, on the eve of the first tryouts in May 1995, Katrina McClain had just decided to accept an offer of $300,000 to play for a club team in Hungary. Because there was still no guarantee of a professional league in the United States, McClain leaned toward returning to Europe. Just two hours before she had to make a decision, she called her brother.

"She supposedly had already made her decision [to take the offer from Hungary]," he said, "but here she was calling me at that late hour, asking advice and second-guessing herself. I knew then what she really wanted to do."

McClain put the contract from the Hungarian team on hold. Like so many others, she still hoped basketball for women would happen in the United States. Maybe this was a way to help jump-start it.

Lisa Leslie could have continued playing in Europe, and also had lucrative modeling contracts. She, too, knew there would have to be sacrifices, both in time and dollars.

"Very little will go on outside of playing basketball right now," she said. "You give up your life when you choose to be with the team for a year."

Teresa Edwards, who had played overseas longer than anyone else—nine years—acknowledged that her whole life revolved around basketball, but felt she could sacrifice overseas earnings to make the sport happen in the United States.

"Basketball was the only game growing up where I could go up against the boys and beat them," she said. "My attitude, the way I perceive things, the way I live my life, has come through basketball. The travel and the different cultures, meeting people and dealing with people, the way I carry myself on and off the court. Everything I could possibly talk about is going to be connected to basketball. I definitely would like to be involved in the growth of this sport here in America on a professional level."

Some of the players just didn't want to go overseas to earn a living anymore. They were willing to give a year to the Olympic effort and hope a pro league would arise in that time. Sheryl Swoopes, for example, played only ten games in Italy in 1993–94 before returning home. After that, she played with various United States all-star teams.

"I know a lot of people who've had great experiences overseas," she said. "Unfortunately, mine wasn't a great one. So that's why I'm so determined to do something to help establish some kind of league in the United States."

Dawn Staley, who played in France, Italy,

Brazil, and Spain, said she was always looking for the opportunity to stay at home.

"A lot of money went toward phone bills and bringing people over to keep me company," she explained. "So staying here now is not that much of a pay cut. Hey, the only reason I played overseas was to get the international experience to help me make [the national team]. Overseas was my sacrifice. This is my reward."

So there was a huge commitment on the part of the players. They saw it as a real opportunity for the sport. There was a feeling in the air that a professional league might be right around the corner. The timing seemed right. If the national team could make its mark and bring home the gold, that just might be enough to make the timing perfect.

It wasn't an easy year. Bringing a team of stars together never is. Tara VanDerveer was a demanding coach. The women learned quickly that there was no room for individual egos. Past success meant nothing. Everyone had to earn her time on the court and think about the team first and foremost. But isn't that the essence of any team sport? Unfortunately, it is often forgotten by today's mega-salaried athletes.

One of the first to suffer the coach's wrath was Rebecca Lobo. The level of play on the national team was a notch or two above the college game, and Lobo was struggling to find her rhythm and her game. At one point, Coach VanDerveer insisted the young forward run two miles in 16 minutes or she wouldn't travel with the team. It took Lobo five tries, but finally she did it.

What made things worse was that Lobo was the main focus of attention at every stop. That was because of all the media coverage she had received at Connecticut. Finally, she spoke about it.

"My teammates know I don't go out seeking any of the craziness that comes along," Lobo said. "It just happens. You just want to go up to people and tell them to watch some of the other girls."

But her teammate and friend Jennifer Azzi said the others never resented the attention given Lobo.

"We love it and we're thankful for it," Azzi

said, "especially that it's aimed at someone of her character. Not many people could handle that kind of exposure. Rebecca's a good ambassador for the sport, and the attention she gets has been helping our team a lot."

The other youngster, Nikki McCray, also got on the wrong side of the tough coach. In one game, when McCray committed several turnovers, VanDerveer told the other women to keep the ball away from her because she didn't know what to do with it. McCray actually began to cry, and her taller teammates gathered around her to shield her from the coach. But in the long run, VanDerveer's tactics allowed everyone to grow as a team and come together emotionally.

"With Tara giving us such hard workouts, we had to pick each other up," Lisa Leslie explained. "We became so close because, at the beginning, it was the coaches versus the team."

Veteran Teresa Edwards also saw the mixture as a winning one. "A team like this needs a dose of everything," she said, "experience, youth, competitiveness. Rebecca and Nikki represent youth. They only needed time and

Basketball Hall of Famer Ann Meyers *(left)*, now a sports commentator, shares her insights during a Liberty vs. Sparks game.

WNBA President Valerie Ackerman shows off the league's new basketball. Two and a half ounces lighter and one inch smaller than the men's ball, it has alternating sections of orange and off-white that make the spin of the ball more visible to fans.

Though many stars from her era felt too old to play, 38-year-old Basketball Hall of Famer Nancy Lieberman-Cline decided to join the Phoenix Mercury in the inaugural season of the WNBA. A native of Brooklyn, New York, she learned the game in city playgrounds and was the first woman to play in a men's professional league.

Arguably the best women's basketball player ever, Cheryl Miller could do it *all*. But with a history of knee problems, she opted to become coach and general manager of the Phoenix Mercury rather than a player in the newly formed WNBA.

Rebecca Lobo—shown here giving an interview—has been the focus of attention wherever she goes. Her New York Liberty teammates don't resent her fame, however. They consider her a good ambassador for the sport.

Rebecca Lobo (6'4") hauls down a rebound against the Sacramento Monarchs.

Forward Nikki McCray of the Columbus Quest was among the league's top scorers in the ABL's first season.

Sheryl Swoopes looks for an open teammate to pass to. She has the distinction of being the first female athlete ever to have a shoe named after her—the Nike "Air Swoopes" basketball shoe.

Lisa Leslie (6'5") of the Los Angeles Sparks in action against the New York Liberty. The tall, elegant Leslie not only is an outstanding basketball player but also has worked as a professional model.

Lisa Leslie signing autographs for some of her many fans.

The first WNBA champions! The Houston Comets celebrate after their 65–51 victory over the Liberty.

Sheryl Swoopes guards Rebecca Lobo during the championship game.

A thrilled Cynthia Cooper accepts her award as league MVP following Houston's victory. Houston head coach Van Chancellor stands to her left.

Cynthia Cooper driving to the basket.

Cynthia Cooper demonstrates the offensive prowess that earned her the title of WNBA Most Valuable Player.

Among the ABL signees was Jackie Joyner-Kersee, Olympic gold medal–winning track and field star. Joyner-Kersee had played basketball as a student at UCLA and wanted to suit up again. She also felt her presence as a sports celebrity could help the league attract new fans.

Dawn Staley—point guard for the Richmond Rage—in action. Basketball superstar Earvin "Magic" Johnson says the WNBA should buy the entire ABL "just to get her."

The Los Angeles Sparks look for an opening against the New York Liberty.

patience."

What did it all mean? Simply this: For the top women basketball players, the sport was now hard work. It could certainly still be fun, but to be a top player you had to expect to be pushed hard, and to push yourself hard. The national team would not only be representing their country at the upcoming Olympic Games, but would be showcasing their talents for those who felt the time was right for a women's professional league. After all, if the pro game for women was about to come to America, all these players would likely become stars.

As the team began playing games, there were some obvious weaknesses. They were not a good long-range-shooting ball club and weren't really consistent beyond the three-point line. In addition, the team had just one legitimate center, Lisa Leslie. The coaches complained she was too thin and had a tendency to get into foul trouble. That prompted them to add former Louisiana Tech star Venus Lacey as a backup center just two months before the Olympics.

But despite all the little negatives, there was

one overriding positive. The team was winning. In fact, they were winning every game they played, whether against college teams or on junkets overseas. They toured China and went to Australia, where Nikki McCray showed her maturity by playing a brilliant defensive game against Australia's star point guard, Michele Timms.

"We're trying to let America know that we want to become the best team to ever play in the Olympics," McCray said.

As the team continued to improve and win, the media coverage increased. The players became more focused. They wanted the gold, but more than that they began getting a sense that this would not be a last hurrah. They would not have to migrate overseas again to play. Things were about to change.

"The great players and the game have always been there," said Dawn Staley. "They just haven't gotten the same level of coverage. America is going to embrace us. The momentum is building as we get closer to the Olympics. It's our time now."

Fans who watched the national team soon

began to realize that these women were doing something that hadn't been done before.

"The national team is blowing college teams out of the water," said Anne Flannery, the director of women's athletics at Spalding. "The next level of play, women's professional basketball, is here. And the public is ready for it."

By the end of July, the team had played everywhere. They even traveled to Russia, where they played on a court so cold that they wore down parkas and gloves on the bench. The big news was that they kept winning. But it was sometimes the little things they did that won them countless thousands of additional fans.

On May 26, the team arrived in Providence, Rhode Island, to play a national team from Cuba. The Americans were in top form, soundly whipping the Cubans, 106–58. As was their habit, they signed many autographs and chatted with young fans when the game ended. Finally, they boarded their bus to start toward yet another destination. As they left the Providence Civic Center, someone noticed a solitary young girl with tears in her eyes literally running after the bus. The players demanded that the driver stop. Despite being tired from the game and the long night, they all left the bus and signed autographs for the youngster.

Said Sheryl Swoopes afterward, "It didn't take but two minutes to turn the saddest girl in Rhode Island into the happiest."

Could you ever imagine a men's professional sports team doing something like that? Maybe 40 years ago. Not now. This was just one of the reasons the public seemed to be taking the team—*and* women's basketball—to heart.

"The women in basketball are playing for the sheer joy and love of the game," said Robin Roberts, an ESPN and ABC commentator. "[It's] something the public recognizes. People are sick of men's pro sports, where millionaires are bickering with billionaires."

Anne Flannery echoed those thoughts. "The developments in men's sports should raise a red flag for all those involved in women's athletics," she said. "We're seeing the fans revolt against the greed in professional sports, and we shouldn't have to do things that way."

Pro basketball, baseball, football, hockey—as played by the men—had lost something as salaries and perks went higher and higher. Gone was team loyalty. Players would most likely offer their services to the highest bidder. Owners tried to get richer. If they didn't like their stadium and the city wouldn't build a new one, they would take their teams elsewhere. Players' unions threatened or went on strikes. Owners sometimes locked the players out, delaying or shortening seasons. In 1994, a baseball players' strike actually caused the cancellation of one of America's most cherished institutions—the World Series.

As the Olympics approached, many fans began looking at women's basketball as a chance for sports to regain some of the purity that had been lost.

Rebecca Lobo spoke for many when she said people liked women's basketball because it was played much the way men's basketball used to be played, with a lot fewer theatrics and a lot more teamwork.

"It's so much more than just flying through the air," she said. "I think it's great that some women can dunk; I wish I was one of them. As long as they don't lose the whole team concept of women's basketball."

Even before the Atlanta Games began in July 1996, it began to appear as if the dream would come true. It was learned that there would be not one but *two* women's professional basketball leagues beginning shortly. The American Basketball League would begin play in October 1996. And a second league, the Women's National Basketball Association, would play its first season beginning in June 1997.

But first things first. What about the dedicated young women who worked for a year to represent their country in the Olympics? When the team arrived in Atlanta on July 17, it had won 52 consecutive games played in seven different countries. The 27 games they had played in the United States drew 162,247 fans, with many, many more watching on television. Ten of the games were televised live.

The players and coaches had also traveled a total of 102,245 miles—the equivalent of four flights around the earth. Between October 2, 1995, and July 17, 1996, the team members had been away from home 240 of 289 days. They all had to be extremely dedicated to make that kind of commitment and sacrifice.

Many of the players had become true celebrities. Members of the team were guests on television shows such as *CBS This Morning, The Charlie Rose Show, CNN This Morning, Good Morning America, The Late Show with David Letterman, Live with Regis & Kathie Lee, The Rosie O'Donnell Show, The Tonight Show,* and *Weekend Today.*

Rebecca Lobo also made a cameo appearance in the film *Jerry Maguire,* while Katrina McClain appeared in an episode of the television sitcom *In the House.* If all that didn't make the team perfect ambassadors for women's basketball, nothing would.

Team USA opened its Olympic schedule with a game against Cuba—a team they had crushed by 48 points back in May. Early on, however, the women must have had a case of the nerves. The Cubans actually had a seven-point lead in the early going. But soon the talent of the United States team took over. With Lisa Leslie scoring 24 points, Sheryl Swoopes 12, and Katy Steding 11, the United States took a 101–84 victory in their opening game.

In their second game, Ruthie Bolton-Holifield had 21 points while Katrina McClain added 17, as the United States topped Ukraine, 98–65. A weak Zaire team fell next, 107–47. Then came a tough test against unbeaten Australia and their star guard, Michele Timms.

With Timms playing very well (she would score a game-high 26), Australia kept it close. The U.S. had just a 46–43 lead after the first half. But then the quartet of McClain (24), Edwards (20), Swoopes (17), and Leslie (16) took charge in the second half to lead the United States to a 96–79 victory. The team had now won four straight and was getting closer to the gold.

Next South Korea fell, as Nikki McCray came off the bench to score 16 points in a 105–64 rout. Now the team was in the quarter-finals against Japan. Once again the Americans shot very well, led by Leslie's USA-record 35 points. McClain scored 18 and tied an Olympic rebounding record with 16. McCray scored 12 points, hitting all five of her shots from the floor, while Teresa Edwards dished out 12 assists. Team USA won,

108–93, and moved into the semi-finals.

This one was a rematch with the Australians. Timms scored 27 points this time, but the Aussies were no match for the balanced United States attack. Five players scored in double figures, led by Leslie's 22, McClain's 18, and Swoopes's 16. McClain also had 15 rebounds, while Leslie grabbed 13. The final score was 93–71.

Now the U.S. would be playing for the gold against another unbeaten team, Brazil. The Brazilians had beaten U.S. teams in the semi-finals of the 1994 World Championships and also in the 1991 Pan American Games. They were a confident bunch.

"We're going to steal the gold medal right in their home," said Brazil's star center, Marta deSouza Sobral.

Tara VanDerveer tried to get her troops ready in another way, prodding them to an even greater performance.

"I can't believe we would come this far and not play our best game," she said.

The United States started the same team that was on the court at the beginning of each game: Edwards and Bolton-Holifield at guards, Leslie at center, Swoopes and McClain at forwards. And this time all the practice, all the work, all the games paid off. The team came out for the biggest game it had ever played and could do no wrong. Playing in front of 32,987 fans at the Georgia Dome, the U.S. jumped in front and was never behind.

Shooting at a 71.9 percent clip (23 of 32) in the first half, the U.S. held a 57–46 lead at intermission. But it was an impressive 8–0 run in the opening minutes of the second half that finished the Brazilians. When the game ended, the United States had an 111–87 victory. They had shot an outstanding 66.2 percent from the field. Better yet, they had won the gold!

After a slow start, Lisa Leslie finished with 29 points, hitting 12 of her 14 shots. Swoopes had 16 points, Bolton-Holifield 15, and McClain 12. Edwards and Staley had 9 apiece, while Edwards also dished out 10 assists. Everyone on the team played and scored. It was truly a team effort.

"Without a doubt, this was our best whole game," a jubilant Coach VanDerveer said.

On the victory stand, the 12 members of the United States team held hands in a gesture of total togetherness. A feeling of "We did it!" was on everyone's mind. Perhaps no national team had ever been closer, no group had ever worked harder for a single goal.

"We accomplished what we set out to do," Lisa Leslie said afterward. "We tried to get women's basketball to the next level."

That turned out to be true. In winning Olympic gold, the women of the United States national team had helped accomplish something special, something all of them had dreamed about for many years. In the upcoming months, they would realize that dream: playing professional basketball before the home fans in the United States.

5 New Leagues, New Attitudes

By the time the Games ended in early August, there was no more doubt about it. There would soon be two professional women's basketball leagues up and running. It was great news for players who had waited a long time. As Olympian Katrina McClain said, "It has to be now....This is our chance to get everybody's attention by showing that we can play and that it's fun to watch women's basketball. People in this country don't realize that the best women's basketball is played *after* college."

The increased acceptance of women's basketball at the college level gave organizers of the new women's leagues plenty of capital to take to the bank. Attendance at NCAA women's Division I regular season games had more than tripled since 1982. Tournament attendance had climbed from 67,000 in 1982 to 248,000 in 1995. The title game between UConn and Tennessee in 1995 had more television viewers than an NBA regular-season game televised at the same time.

Finally, the success of the national team had proved once and for all that the quality of the women's game could be even better. The Olympians had rolled over the college teams they played against. They had taken women's basketball to a higher level than had ever been seen before in the United States. The players became personalities and celebrities. Now *two* groups thought the time had come for women's basketball to have its own stage. The two leagues—the American Basketball League and the Women's National Basketball Association—would go about the business of basketball in very different ways. Both, however, had one thing in common. They wanted to put the best possible product on the court and in front of the fans.

The Leagues

The American Basketball League started play first. They would have a 40-game season between October 1996 and February 1997 with the playoffs running into early March. That would overlap the normal college and professional hoop seasons. The league started with eight teams—the Atlanta (Georgia) Glory, the (Denver) Colorado Xplosion, the Columbus (Ohio) Quest, the New England (Hartford, Connecticut, and Springfield, Massachusetts) Blizzard, the Portland (Oregon) Power, the Richmond (Virginia) Rage, the San Jose (California) Lasers, and the Seattle (Washington) Reign.

While the locations chosen were places with a strong interest in women's basketball, the games would be played in small and mid-sized arenas. The founders of the league—Gary Cavalli, Steve Hams, and Anne Cribbs—would be working on a budget that was very modest by the standards of today's sports world. They began with $3 million in seed money and acquired an additional $6 million from two private investors. That might seem like a lot of money, but it isn't when you consider everything that goes into running a brand-new league.

The ABL decided to concentrate on getting the best players it could. Salaries would average in the $70,000-to-$80,000-a-year range, with a few select players getting up to $125,000. That was still far less than the top players could make in Europe, but they didn't mind. Getting a chance to play at home made the sacrifice worthwhile.

With more money being spent on salaries, the ABL wouldn't have a lot left over for marketing. As CEO Gary Cavalli explained, the marketing effort would be grass-roots. Players would do a lot of public relations work in person, appearing at shopping malls and other places where large numbers of people were. They would sign autographs, talk to people about basketball and the ABL, and invite them to come to the games.

"Not having a big war chest, we plan to take the product to the consumer," Cavalli said.

The league owned all eight teams and went into its initial season fully prepared to lose up to $4 million the first year. As with any new business, a loss is not uncommon for a new league. But the ABL hoped to continue to attract top players by allowing them to own ten percent of the league in the form of a Players' Trust. The players would also have a voice in league management via an advisory board.

Individual team operators would independently manage their teams and hire needed personnel. They would also draft and trade players, negotiate local contracts, and be responsible for marketing their teams.

The WNBA, by contrast, was a well-oiled, well-financed league. It was being bankrolled by the highly successful, very wealthy National Basketball Association. In effect, it was the NBA's sister league. Each team was owned by the corresponding NBA team in its city, and the WNBA teams played in the NBA arenas. There was also a $15 million allocation for promoting and publicizing the league.

The WNBA would not play during the traditional basketball season, and thus would not go head-to-head with the ABL. The first WNBA season would consist of 28 games, to be played between June 21 and August 30, 1996, when the title game would take place.

There were eight WNBA teams in the league's first year. The Eastern Conference consisted of the Charlotte (North Carolina) Sting, the Cleveland (Ohio) Rockers, the Houston (Texas) Comets, and the New York (New York City) Liberty. These teams were directly affiliated with the NBA Charlotte Hornets, the Cleveland Cavaliers, the Houston Rockets, and the New York Knicks. The Western Conference WNBA entries were the Los Angeles (California) Sparks, the Phoenix (Arizona) Mercury, the Sacramento (California) Monarchs, and the Utah Starzz. Their NBA counterparts were the Los Angeles Lakers, the Phoenix Suns, the Sacramento Kings, and the Utah Jazz.

It didn't take long for the WNBA to pick up corporate sponsors and network television contracts. Being affiliated with the NBA did that. The WNBA's emphasis was on marketing, and the players' average salary was about $40,000, less than that of the ABL. Of course, there were several major stars making much more. But the difference would be made up in marketing and exposure.

It was apparent there would be competition between the leagues. It was hoped that both would survive.

"We feel that women's basketball is a great sport that deserves to stand on a stage of its own during the traditional basketball season," the ABL's Gary Cavalli explained. "You really have two totally different strategies here, and I don't know who's right and who's wrong. It could be that both of us are right, and two leagues will survive."

Cavalli was referring to the WNBA playing its games during the summer months, away from the traditional season, while the ABL decided to go with the flow and play during everyone else's basketball season. Maybe, however, that set-up would give the two leagues a better chance at survival.

Both wanted to offer affordable entertainment. Individual tickets to ABL games averaged about $10 a seat, with select courtside seats in the $25–$35 range. The WNBA tickets were roughly the same, with some special bargains thrown in. In Charlotte, for instance, a family of four could buy a "Valupak." That would provide four tickets, four hot dogs, four sodas, and popcorn, all for $25. By contrast, it can cost a family several hundred dollars to attend a regular-season NBA game.

Both the ABL and WNBA knew that public acceptance would determine if their leagues survived. They both planned on doing all they could to build a fan base. And that included giving their players all the exposure they could.

The Players

There was a kind of irony in the ABL-WNBA situation. For years there had been no professional basketball league for women in the United States. Now, suddenly, there were two. The good part was that there would be twice as many jobs available. But there would also be competition for the best players. Fans waited to see where their favorites would go.

Because its season would begin just two

months after the Olympics ended, they needed to sign players quickly. This gave them something of a jump on the WNBA. As it turned out, eight of the twelve women on the U.S. Olympic team signed with the ABL. That group included Teresa Edwards, Katrina McClain, Dawn Staley, Jennifer Azzi, and Nikki McCray. McClain, however, had to honor a commitment in Europe and wouldn't start her ABL career until 1997.

But the WNBA scored a coup as well. They signed Lisa Leslie, Rebecca Lobo, and Sheryl Swoopes, the three players with perhaps the most corporate marketability. They would become major spokeswomen for the new league. A short time later, the league also signed Olympian Ruthie Bolton-Holifield.

After that, there was a rash of signings, with both current college graduates and former players joining the new leagues. Many returned from overseas to play at home, while those fresh out of college jumped at the chance to play professionally. A few foreign players were also recruited to play, something that had never happened before.

The ABL signed Brazilian star Marta de-

Souza Sobral, who had played against the U.S. in the Olympic gold medal game. The WNBA had Australian point guard Michele Timms, as well as Elena Baranova of Russia, Mikiko Hagiwara of Japan, Zheng Haixia of China, Isabelle Fijalkowski of France, and Janeth Arcain of Brazil all in the fold.

In addition, the WNBA signed all-time legends Lynette Woodard and Nancy Lieberman-Cline. Both were nearing 40 years of age but wanted one last chance to play professionally in the United States. And among the ABL signees was Jackie Joyner-Kersee, one of America's greatest track and field athletes.

Joyner-Kersee had once played basketball at UCLA before becoming the first woman to win back-to-back Olympic gold medals in a grueling track and field event, the heptathlon (seven different track and field events that take place on two consecutive days). Now she said she wanted to get the feel of playing a team sport again. She also felt her presence as a sports celebrity could help the league and the sport gather new fans.

"I hope the ABL will be a success," she said.

"Even the [WNBA]—I hope they will be a success, too. And if one league is not to survive, hopefully both leagues can consolidate so they can continue to open doors for young girls who dream of playing professional basketball."

Some players were forced to take a leave of absence from other professions to return to basketball. Sonja Henning of the ABL San Jose Lasers was a practicing attorney. Lynette Woodard was a registered stockbroker. Ruthie Bolton-Holifield was a first lieutenant in the Army Reserves.

But all the women were basketball players, and their comments revealed how long they had waited for this to happen. Trish Roberts had played in the Women's Professional Basketball League back in 1979. When she heard about the ABL, she wanted to do her part, and became coach of the Atlanta Glory.

"When they announced they were going to form this league, I was skeptical," Roberts said. "I had seen too many leagues come and go. But the ABL was a year in the making, and they used that whole year preceding the Olympics to prepare, to form the league and put their policies and goals into place. It's not where it should be, but it's a start...and it's going to go in the right direction."

Olympic star Teresa Edwards, another great veteran player, saw the pro leagues as an opportunity to create a whole new generation of role models for girls. It was Edwards who coined the ABL's slogan, "Little girls need big girls to look up to!"

"As a kid, I loved Dr. J [Julius Erving] and then grew to love Michael Jordan," she said. "But I can't perform like them; my body will not allow me to do the things that their bodies will. If there had been a woman in that position, I could have aspired to be like her."

Lynette Woodard, who would be a WNBA rookie at the age of 37, looked back at her long career and said, "I've been extremely lucky...I have a gift to play the game, and I didn't believe God would have given me one piece of the puzzle and not the other. Every time it appeared there was no more, I kept working and there was another opportunity. The WNBA continues that pattern."

For Sheryl Swoopes, playing professionally

in her own country would be the pinnacle of her career. "A national championship, a gold medal—all of those are very important and mean a lot to me. But to finally have an opportunity to do something I've wanted to do since I was seven, eight years old—and that is to stay in my own country and play professional basketball—to have an opportunity to do that is definitely exciting.

"We had to watch little girls looking for basketball role models and asking their parents to buy them jerseys with [Michael] Jordan and [Charles] Barkley and [Grant] Hill on them. I understand the popularity of the NBA players, but it hurt a little bit that we did not have the opportunity to be role models for little girls with dreams of playing professional basketball. But now I think we have that chance."

Rebecca Lobo saw the rise of the women's game as more than just a league where women could play.

"We're excited," she said. "But it's not just about us. It's about women being in TV commercials for professional leagues. It's about so much energy and enthusiasm for the start of this league. It's about all the women—not just me—and that's very gratifying and exciting."

Swoopes spoke for many when she admitted how envious the women players had been of their male counterparts over the years.

"We would sit home and watch the [NBA] draft, and we'd see the men getting their caps and everything when they knew what team they were going to. It's great to see we're having the same opportunity."

Swoopes, however, also symbolized another side of the women's game. The side that could only be experienced by women athletes. She would not be playing at the outset of the WNBA season because she and her husband, Eric Jackson, were expecting their first child in June 1997. At first, Swoopes was concerned that having a child might not only affect her play when she returned but also the way the league marketed her talents.

"I thought all my sponsors wouldn't want me anymore," she said.

But this was women's sports. Pregnancy was a part of life and was accepted without question.

"We embrace maternity," said Rick Welts,

the chief marketing officer for both the NBA and the WNBA.

Sure enough, Swoopes's pregnancy would be followed closely, and the birth of her son—aptly named Jordan—became a celebrated WNBA event. Women's basketball, it was apparent, was prepared for any contingency.

But perhaps the player who best symbolized what the advent of women's professional basketball really meant was Cynthia Cooper. Born in 1963 in Chicago, Illinois, Cooper didn't start playing basketball until she was 16 years old. At Locke High School in Los Angeles she not only played basketball but also ran track and played volleyball, softball, and badminton.

She then played basketball for four years at USC, where she was part of the national championship teams in 1983 and 1984. Cooper became a fine college player, averaging 12.9 points a game for her career. But she wasn't an All-American and wasn't considered one of the best players in the country.

Cooper, however, loved the game and didn't quit. She played on the United States national team in two World Championships (1986 and

1990) and two Olympics (1988 and 1992). She also played 11 seasons in Spain and Italy, where she refined her game and became a top scorer. During her final eight years overseas, Cooper averaged 30.5 points a game.

When the WNBA was formed, Cooper finally got the chance to come home. At age 34, the 5'10" guard joined the Houston Comets without much fanfare. She wasn't expected to become a superstar in the new league, but she had always kept herself in top physical condition and had never stopped working on her game.

"I didn't think at age 34 my body would feel this good, but I've always said that I'm going to play as long as my body allowed me to," she explained. "But I feel good. I could play three, four, five more years. When my body says that's enough, it's going to be *enough*."

The veteran players seemed to get a new lease on life when the ABL and WNBA came along. They had, after all, been waiting for this chance practically all their lives. When the two leagues began play, it was as if all the players were 21 again.

The Game

Finally, it was time for the hype to stop and the games to begin. It would be the final test. If the women didn't put an exciting product on the floor, both leagues would go the way of the previous efforts to sell women's pro basketball. That was the bottom line. The product had to appeal to the public. All the groundwork had been laid. It was time for the players to perform.

Bear in mind that the ABL season began in October 1996 and ran until March 1997. The WNBA season started in June 1997 and was completed at the end of August.

The ABL opened with much less hype than the WNBA would. Nevertheless, three teams (Atlanta, San Jose, and Seattle) sold out on opening night. New England and Portland each drew more than 8,700 fans to their openers. Attendance at the smaller ABL arenas would level off somewhat and average just over 3,500 fans per game for the season. Yet this was some 20 percent higher than the league's pre-season projections.

And no one could complain about the style of game being played. There were tight, pass-oriented offenses and solid, hardworking defenses. Unlike the men, the women played below the rim, so the game resembled the pure basketball of earlier times. No one was flying through the air for a monster jam. Many purists soon said they liked the women's game better than the men's. One of those was John Wooden, who had coached UCLA to ten NCAA titles.

"The women's game is simply more watchable," Wooden said.

The ABL soon found it had one super team that was dominating the league. The Columbus Quest would win 18 of its first 19 games. The Quest were playing with such confidence and style that they were already being called one of the best women's teams in the world. And, in a number of ways, they were the first symbols of what the women's game was all about, both in its triumphs and in its problems.

The Quest had a number of outstanding players, beginning with forward Nikki McCray, who had been on the Olympic team. She was more than amply supported by Katie Smith, who had been an All-American the year before at nearby Ohio State; guards Shannon "Pee Wee" Johnson and Tonya "Ice" Edwards; forward Andrea Lloyd; and 35-year-old forward/center Valerie Still. Each of them could play the game with style. McCray, Smith, and Edwards were among the league's top scorers.

This was a team that played a cohesive, "together" game. They often ran the fast break, an exciting maneuver that was all but forgotten in the men's professional game. In fact, the Quest ran about a dozen fast breaks per game, racing the ball upcourt, pushing the tempo. And when they didn't run a break, the Quest would set double and triple picks. (A pick is when an offensive player stands still on the court, allowing the ball handler to cut directly behind her, "picking off" the defensive players. It's a tried-and-true way to get a shot off, and the Quest were very good at it.)

The players were hardworking and intense on defense, often diving for loose balls and contesting every shot. In fact, that kind of effort quickly became part of all ABL teams.

"The one thing I hear most from fans and

sportwriters," said league CEO Gary Cavalli, "is that they can't think of any other league where the players play so hard from the tip to the end of the game."

That effort could be seen in the play of veteran Valerie Still. She had played in Italy for 12 long years and wasn't sure whether she could still compete with much younger women in a faster game.

"The European game is more physical," Still said, "but there's more athleticism here. I watched the young girls coming up on television, and I didn't know if I could compete, as old as I am. I just have to get here earlier and start warming up before the others."

Still was called on to start in games against Colorado and New England when Andrea Lloyd sat out with a sprained knee. She responded by scoring 24 points and grabbing 15 rebounds in an inspired performance.

"At my age I'm not going to get nervous out there," she said. "I've got a kid at home who might have a fever and a husband who might complain that I'm not cooking enough. When we go on the road, it's like a free pass."

The women certainly looked at things differently. There was no bickering over million-dollar contracts, no jealousy, and no prima donnas. The Columbus Quest seemed to symbolize just what women's pro basketball could be.

But what about the problems? Despite being the best team in the league, the Quest were having difficulty picking up a fan base. Columbus is a huge football town, and many fans would rather follow the gridiron exploits of the Ohio State University Buckeyes. And when football season ends, there are the Buckeye basketball teams, both the men's and women's. After 13 home games, the Quest were averaging just 2,452 fans, some 900 below the league average. Battelle Hall, where the team played, had a seating capacity of 6,700, but the Quest weren't coming close to filling it up.

"I don't know who will ever arrive in this town as a professional team and take anything away from the Buckeyes," said Katie Smith, who played for Ohio State just a year earlier.

Yet there were already some diehard fans. And that's what the league was hoping for—people who would keep coming back and also spread the word.

Ebony Pegues, a point guard at local Eastmoor High in Columbus, hadn't missed a single Quest game.

"It's so competitive," she said, adding that her high school teammates all studied the court action and the players to try to improve their own games.

There were those who worried that once the WNBA began, with its big-money marketing machine, the ABL might be swallowed up. As one regular fan said, "No women's league has ever flown, and now we'll have two. And we all know the NBA has the money."

But all in all, the ABL got off to a good start. The brand of basketball was solid and there was a hard-core fan base already established. Players like Nikki McCray, Teresa Edwards, Dawn Staley, Debbie Black, Jennifer Rizzotti, Carolyn Jones, and Tonya Edwards had already shown that the new league had some fine all-around talent. Everyone agreed that, overall, the caliber of play was excellent.

One local resident and new Quest fan often brought his wife and two young children to the games. As did many others, he liked not only his local team but the women's game as a whole. And he spoke for many fans who would voice similar thoughts in the upcoming months. "I like the women's game better than the men's. It's less glitz and more no-nonsense basketball."

When the WNBA started up the following June, the splash was much bigger and noisier. With NBA money and sponsorship behind it, the WNBA was hyped to the hilt. The league even unveiled a new basketball. It was two and a half ounces lighter and one inch smaller than the men's ball. It was the same size used for women at the high school and college level, but not in international play, where the regular men's ball was used. In addition, the WNBA ball had alternating sections of orange and off-white. That made the spin of the ball more visible to the fans.

"We think it's an exciting element," said Kelly Krauskopf, WNBA director of basketball operations. "It's a distinctive look, and fans seem to enjoy watching the rotation of the ball on even the most routine shot or pass. It brings another dimension to our game."

While the ABL began with very little television exposure, the WNBA had contracts with three networks—ESPN, Lifetime, and NBC. Plus they were opening up in major NBA arenas, where everyone knew how to put on a pregame show, complete with laser light displays. Press coverage was also at a much higher level. But, as was the case with the ABL, the final product would come under a critical eye.

There was some concern about the readiness of the players. For one thing, the teams had just three weeks of pre-season play—not much time for new teammates to get to know one another. In addition, the slightly smaller ball was new to most of the players. Many of the veterans had been using the larger ball for years overseas.

The league opened play on Saturday, June 21, with a game between its two marquee teams—the Los Angeles Sparks with Lisa Leslie and the New York Liberty with Rebecca Lobo. Some 14,284 fans arrived at the Great Western Forum in Los Angeles to watch this first-ever WNBA game. In the opening minute, Sparks guard Penny Toler went around the Liberty's Vickie Johnson and hit a short jump shot, the first points ever scored in the new league.

After that, play got a little ragged. The Sparks didn't really have the spark, and the Liberty went on to win 67–57. At one point in the game, 6'5" Leslie had the ball out in front on a break. Being perhaps the only WNBA player who can dunk, she tried to jam one home, but the ball thudded off the front rim.

"Dunking is not part of my game," Leslie said later. "I can dunk, but...I didn't make it. I was kind of coming downcourt thinking, 'Do I do it, do I not do it?' And I kind of ran into the rim."

Instead, Rebecca Lobo and the Liberty prevailed. In the battle between the two high-profile players, Leslie had 16 points and 14 rebounds, while Lobo scored 16 and grabbed 6 boards. But the Liberty won the game, and Lobo was ecstatic.

"When you've been dreaming about it for the past year, it's almost like an out-of-body experience," Lobo said. "Even now to think about the game, it's a clutter in my mind. I think it opened a lot of people's eyes to our athletic talent.

"At the same time, I'm glad this game is behind us. Now we can calm down and play the way we *can* play the game. It wasn't a pretty game. I think everyone had jitters."

The other WNBA openers were just as encouraging in terms of attendance. In Phoenix, a huge crowd of 16,102 fans jammed the America West Arena (capacity: 19,063) as the hometown Mercury—coached by legend Cheryl Miller—defeated the Charlotte Sting 76–59. Bridget Pettis scored 17 for Phoenix, while Andrea Stinson had 18 for Charlotte, as the fans got used to rooting for new heroes.

At one point in the game, the Sting had closed the Phoenix lead to 35–26 when all-time legend Nancy Lieberman-Cline hit a clutch three-pointer to stop the Charlotte run. Less than two weeks from her 39th birthday, Lieberman-Cline showed she was still a player to be reckoned with.

More openers: In Cleveland, 11,455 fans were at the Gund Arena to see 34-year-old Cynthia Cooper score 25 points for the Houston Comets as they topped the Rockers, 76–56. And with 8,915 fans at the Delta Center in Salt Lake

City, Ruthie Bolton-Holifield had 18 points as her Sacramento club eclipsed the Starzz, 70–60.

The first four WNBA games had drawn more than 50,000 fans, exceeding all expectations. The Sparks-Liberty opener on NBC outdrew regional baseball telecasts on Fox, a PGA golf tournament on CBS, and an auto race on ABC.

Everyone seemed overjoyed. The players, coaches, league officials, TV networks, and corporate sponsors all gushed about the huge crowds.

"Are you as amazed as I am that we're drawing 12,000 here tonight?" said Houston coach Van Chancellor. "Never in my wildest dreams did I see *this* happening."

Despite her team's loss, Lisa Leslie was also beaming. "They were even cheering for free throws," she said. "We were overwhelmed by it."

There was, however, one thing that was overlooked amidst all the early optimism. Despite some great individual performances, overall play was a bit sloppy. The L.A. Sparks, for instance, shot just 31 percent and had 25 turnovers. That would have to improve quickly if the league expected the fans to keep coming out.

The WNBA learned very quickly that it had better raise its level of play. Because the ABL season had already ended by the time the WNBA began, there would be comparisons. That was just human nature. Mel Greenberg, who started the first nationwide women's basketball poll in 1976 and had followed the game closely ever since, immediately looked at the WNBA teams in terms of the ABL.

"I'd say Phoenix and Charlotte could play in the ABL right now and do well," he said. But Greenberg also pointed out that the ABL had signed recent college stars Kara Wolters of UConn and Stanford's Kate Starbird for their second season.

"The ABL already has the two best college

players from 1996–97," Greenberg said, "and other ABL signings took the heart of the strong Southeastern Conference."

Could it be that the players were already going for the higher salaries of the ABL against the marketing promise and large league bankroll of the WNBA? Only time would tell.

One of basketball's greatest players, Earvin "Magic" Johnson, had attended the Sparks-Liberty opener. Magic felt that the women should be playing four 12-minute quarters, as in the NBA. He felt that two 20-minute halves—college length—wasn't enough.

"These are professional women," Magic said. "They can play longer than college. They need to make it 12-minute quarters. Then you'd get more excitement, because the game is longer."

The Magic Man also felt there wasn't enough talent for two leagues and thought a merger of the two leagues would be in the best interest of the women's game. As an example, he looked at his old position, point guard, saying that the top performer at this critical position was in the ABL.

"The WNBA needs Dawn Staley," Magic

said. "She's a showstopper. She's what it's all about: no-look, behind-the-back, through-the-legs. They should buy that league just to get her."

But there was no talk of a merger. Both leagues already had plans to expand on their own. And the WNBA continued to do what it had planned—market their product relentlessly. When the Liberty debuted at Madison Square Garden in New York on June 29, there were a record 17,780 fans in the building to watch. It was the largest crowd ever to watch a women's pro basketball game in the United States. And the fans got what they came for as the Liberty toppled Phoenix, 65–57. The New York backcourt of point guard Teresa Weatherspoon and shooting guard Sophie Witherspoon (known as "T-Spoon" and "Serving Spoon") thrilled the crowd with their exciting play.

At one point, Weatherspoon saved the ball just as it was going out of bounds. As she fell, she threw an acrobatic, behind-the-head pass to Witherspoon, who went in for a layup. The crowd went berserk. This was the kind of excitement the league was looking for. The game stayed close until the final minutes, when Witherspoon hit a layup and a free throw to bring the lead to 63–57. Witherspoon had 14 points, while Lobo scored 13 and grabbed 8 rebounds. Guard Vickie Johnson led the team with 20 points, while center Jennifer Gillom had 23 for the Mercury.

The Liberty were now 4–0 and building quite a following in New York. Girls could be seen wearing Liberty T-shirts that also had the "We got next!" slogan on them. And there were plenty of families at the game, too.

John Bennett and his wife drove two hours from their Long Island home to take their nine-year-old daughter to the game.

"She got into [women's basketball] by watching the women's Final Four this year. I think that really did it for her," Bennett said. He also brought up something else about the game, something other families were noticing.

"I can't afford the hundreds of dollars it costs to come to the [NBA] Knicks games," he said. "This is professional sports, it's affordable, and it's good basketball."

WNBA president Val Ackerman was happy

about the initial response to the league, but he was still cautious.

"We are being very realistic about all of this," she said. "We don't expect to sustain the crowds of 15,000 and 16,000 we have had in Sacramento and Phoenix. But the interest is there. It certainly bodes well for the future of the sport."

At the same time play began to improve on the court, the players also did their best to make the fans part of the game. The teams held clinics for underprivileged kids and signed autographs for their fans. After a loss to the Liberty, Charlotte Sting player Vicky Bullett was signing autographs for young fans who had waited to meet the players. Before leaving, she asked, "Have I missed anyone?" Imagine an NBA or major league baseball player doing that.

At another game, guard Rhonda Blades of the Liberty was kneeling alongside the scorer's table, waiting to enter the game, when she spotted two little girls sitting courtside.

"Just before Rhonda went into the game," said Val Ackerman, "she turned and gave one of the girls a high-five. Then the girl showed her hand to her friend, as if she had been given this wonderful present. And I guess she had."

During a fan appreciation night at the Garden, one of the regular ushers noticed something special happen.

"At one point," he said, "a girl told Teresa Weatherspoon that she was her hero, and Teresa went right up into the stands to give her a hug. Somehow I don't envision [Knicks star] Patrick Ewing doing that."

After the Phoenix home opener, Australian point guard Michele Timms spent two hours signing autographs. The next day she wrote a letter to the *Arizona Republic,* apologizing for not being able to sign for every last person.

Another popular young WNBA player was Jamila Wideman, a rookie with the L.A. Sparks. The 5'6" guard had been a standout performer at Stanford University, where she earned a degree in both political science and African-American studies. Jamila is the daughter of Pulitzer Prize–winning author John Edgar Wideman. Her mother, Judy, graduated from law school at age 51. Jamila had had to deal with tremendous pressures after her 16-year-old brother killed another teen and was sentenced to life in prison. Because of her father's celebrity, the story received widespread publicity.

Yet on the basketball court she is just another hardworking player, giving her all to make it as a pro.

"[The other players] are women I grew up hearing about but never got a chance to see play," she said. "Now, not only do I get to see them play, I have to guard them."

Jamila's spirited play and personal story made her such a positive role model that the Sparks often received more appearance requests for her than for the team's star, Lisa Leslie.

As the WNBA season continued, more human-interest stories about the players emerged. Ruthie Bolton-Holifield of the Sacramento Monarchs was always willing to take the brunt of the pressure for her teammates. The 30-year-old veteran, a member of the Army Reserves, grew up in a family of 20 children. She joked that "even just sitting around the house, we'd end up five on a couch designed for four. So we *had* to get along."

She also had the amazing total of 72 nieces and nephews. That's a lot of people looking up to "Aunt Ruthie."

Bolton-Holifield would average close to 20 points a game all year. "I actually put a lot of pressure on myself," she said. "If we are behind by ten, I want to get us back in with one shot."

Having married Mark Holifield in 1991, Ruthie has talked about one day taking time out from her career to have a child. That's something else you wouldn't hear in the NBA.

Liberty guard Teresa Weatherspoon was a 31-year-old veteran who had been an All-American at Louisiana Tech and member of the national championship team in 1988. After that, she played eight years overseas. Everything she had done, learned, and seen had an impact on her life. She remembered hitting a clutch shot as a freshman at Louisiana Tech, a shot that sent a game against Cheryl Miller and USC into overtime.

"The moment I went with my decision to shoot the ball, I grew as a player."

Weatherspoon also studied her history and related it to what she and the other women were doing now.

"Jackie Robinson (the first African-American to play major league baseball) once said, 'Your life is successful when you have an impact on another life,'" Weatherspoon related. "I find that very motivational because we have the opportunity to do that."

Despite her philosophical outlook, Weatherspoon is one of the most aggressive, combative players in the league. She fights a battle every minute she is in the game.

"When I play you on defense," she said, "I love when you look me in the eye. I'm attacking. I think about being the aggressor at all times. And I always play better after I get a hit on me."

So the WNBA got off to a strong start, interacted with its fans, and marketed its players. It all boded well for a first-year league. President Val Ackerman sounded quite pleased. Women's basketball "has never had this level of exposure before, or the track records of all the NBA organizations behind us."

But it was a sports buyer for a major ad agency in New York who sounded a cautionary note.

"I don't see any liabilities," the man said. "I see a growth factor. But whether the novelty wears off in the second year, nobody knows."

The Home Stretch

By the second half of both the ABL and WNBA seasons, the novelty had worn off. The two leagues were still trying to spread the word and do the best marketing job they could. But for the players now, the game was the thing. There was a much stronger sense of team than there had been early in the season. Players knew one another better, both on and off the court. Like all professional athletes, everyone wanted to win.

In the ABL, the Columbus Quest finished with the league's best record at 31–9. They were ten games ahead of the 21–19 Richmond Rage in the Eastern Conference. In the West, the Colorado Xplosion were on top at 25–15. The five other teams all had sub-.500 records, though the San Jose Lasers also made the playoffs (with an 18–22 mark).

Carolyn Jones of New England was the first

ABL scoring champion, with a 21.2 average. Veteran Teresa Edwards was still great, finishing second at 21.1 points per game, while young Nikki McCray was third at 19.9. Natalie Williams of Portland led all rebounders, grabbing 12.5 a game, while Magic Johnson's favorite point guard, Dawn Staley, led in assists, with 8 per game.

The All-ABL first team consisted of Edwards and Staley at the guards, Natalie Williams at center, and McCray and Adrienne Goodson of Richmond at the forwards. McCray was the league's first Most Valuable Player, winning in a close vote over Teresa Edwards.

In the playoffs, Columbus defeated San Jose, while Richmond defeated Colorado. Both won their best-of-three series in two straight games. Now Richmond and Columbus met for the ABL championship in a best-of-five showdown.

It was exciting basketball. Columbus won the first game, 90–89, as McCray hit the winning basket with just under 40 seconds left. Tonya Edwards had 26 points for Columbus, while Richmond converted an incredible 34 of 35 free throws. In Game Two, however, the

Rage upset the Quest in Columbus, winning 75–62 behind 21 points and 17 rebounds from Taj McWilliams.

Then Richmond returned to its home court and won Game Three, 72–67, with McWilliams scoring 20 points. Veteran Valerie Still had 23 for Columbus, but the Quest had their backs against the wall. They would have to win Game Four in Richmond to force a fifth and final contest. That they did, taking a 95–84 shootout behind Katie Smith's 25 points, as all five Columbus starters scored in double figures.

The dramatic championship game was held at a sold-out Battelle Hall on March 11, 1997. The Quest had been the best ABL team all year and didn't want to blow it. Playing with great intensity, they took control early. Led by Tonya Edwards with 23 points and with the defense of Valerie Still, they cruised to a 77–64 victory. Dawn Staley had 19 points in a losing effort.

Valerie Still, the 35-year-old veteran who wasn't sure if she could keep up with the speed of the young players after a long career in Europe, surprised everyone. She averaged 14 points and 8 rebounds during the final series and turned in a sparkling defensive job on high-scoring Taj McWilliams in the final two games. For her efforts, she was named the Most Valuable Player in the finals.

It was a storybook ending to the first-ever American Basketball League season. The league had averaged 4,468 fans during the playoffs and already was planning to add an expansion team for its second year.

The ABL arguably had just as thrilling a first season as the WNBA. There were many individual stories, such as the great play of veterans Teresa Edwards and Valerie Still; the emergence of Dawn Staley as perhaps the most exciting point guard in the women's game; and the rapid development of young Nikki McCray as MVP.

What the ABL didn't have, though, was the huge public relations machine that the WNBA had in place from day one. Coupled with their TV contracts and NBA connection, the WNBA received many times the press coverage, magazine stories, TV interviews, product endorsements, and overall hype. But if all this helped the WNBA, it also helped women's basketball. And so, by association, it helped the ABL.

The WNBA also had the celebrity factor. People like actor/dancer Gregory Hines, actress/talk show hostess Rosie O'Donnell, supermodel Tyra Banks, and actress/director Penny Marshall were among the regulars at WNBA games in New York and Los Angeles.

As the WNBA season unfolded, all kinds of substories appeared. For example, when the New York Liberty ran their record to 5–0, someone pointed out that Rebecca Lobo had not been on a losing team for 100 straight games. That included her 35–0 senior season at the University of Connecticut, followed by the national team's 60–0 run that ended with Olympic gold. Her personal winning streak became a story. Then the Liberty won twice more, making the team 7–0 and Lobo 102–0. Finally, the team lost a 69–50 game to the Mercury. Lobo's streak was over, but she didn't want to hear that.

"It just feels awful to lose," she said, "streak or no streak. We wanted to be 8–0. My streak never crossed my mind until you guys [the press] started mentioning it. I wasn't worried about it. Right now, all I want to do is start another streak."

Though Lobo received the bulk of the media attention, the Liberty were a well-balanced team, with the leader undoubtedly the tenacious Teresa Weatherspoon. Carol Blazejowski, the Liberty general manager, called Weatherspoon "the heart and soul of our team."

"Most of our games are close," said Liberty coach Nancy Darsch, "but this team's poise just takes over, and we beat people with attitude and aggressiveness."

Backing up Lobo at center was 30-year-old Sue Wicks, a star at Rutgers in the late 1980s. Like so many other veterans, Wicks had spent years playing in Europe. She spoke for the other veterans when she said, "When you score 40 points a night in Italy and you lose and you're alone, it's an empty, ugly feeling. The veteran players on this team don't want to be stars anymore. We just want to win. We've all been holding out as long as we could to go out winners in this sport. And nobody on this team is going to blow that opportunity."

Then, as the season moved into its final weeks, a new team and a new superstar began taking center stage from the Liberty. They were the Houston Comets and Cynthia Cooper. The 34-year-old guard and veteran of European play was emerging as not only the best but also the most electrifying player in the league.

Cooper had been in a shooting slump early in the season as the Comets got off to a mediocre 5–4 start. She would take some 300 to 500 jump shots in practice each day until she began to feel her release and shot coming back. Finally, in mid-July, Comets coach Van Chancellor told Cooper she was going to be the team's go-to player. With that vote of confidence, Cooper went out and suddenly became the WNBA's version of Michael Jordan.

In the next three games, she set and broke the league's single-game scoring mark each time out. First it was a 30-point night against Sacramento. That was followed by a 32-point performance against the Phoenix Mercury. Then she topped it off with an incredible 44-point outburst in a rematch with the Sacramento Monarchs. She would score 30 or more points in seven of the 13 Comets games after the talk with her coach. The team won all seven and surged past the fading Liberty into first place.

"I never felt like I had given all I was capable of giving to one of my teams," Cooper said. "I was always the sort of player who was asked to pass the ball to the marquee players and set picks, run the fast break. My role might be to come into the game to be a defensive stopper, or a spark plug. But all along, I told myself, this is not my game. This is not who I am as a basketball player. And this is not all I can do."

The Comets received another shot in the arm on August 7, when Sheryl Swoopes returned to the lineup. She had given birth to her son, Jordan, on June 25, and was working her way back into playing shape. Meanwhile, Cynthia Cooper continued to play like gangbusters.

When the regular season ended, Houston had taken the Eastern Conference with an 18–10 record. The Liberty were second at 17–11. Phoenix won in the West with a 16–10 mark. L.A. was next at 14–14. Charlotte in the East became the fourth playoff team by virtue of its 15–13 final mark.

Cooper was the league's scoring leader, with a 22.2 average, followed by Ruthie Bolton-Holifield at 19.4 and Lisa Leslie with 15.9 points per game. Leslie was the rebounding leader, with 9.5 per game, while Teresa Weatherspoon was tops in assists, with 6.1 per contest. Weatherspoon also led in steals, with 3.04 per game, just ahead of Michele Timms of Phoenix. Timms also tied for second in assists at 5.1.

The All-League team had Eva Nemcova of Cleveland and Tina Thompson of Houston at forwards, Leslie at center, with Cooper and Bolton-Holifield at guards. Van Chancellor was Coach of the Year, while Teresa Weatherspoon was named Defensive Player of the Year. Weatherspoon also headed up the All-League second team, joined by Wendy Palmer of Utah and Rebecca Lobo at forwards, Jennifer Gillom of Phoenix at center, and Andrea Stinson at the other guard.

When the first WNBA Most Valuable Player was chosen, it came as no surprise. Cynthia Cooper was an easy winner.

As an added note, 37-year-old Lynette Woodard—whose long basketball career included a stint with the Harlem Globetrotters—showed she could still play the game. She started 27 of 28 games for the Cleveland Rockers, averaging 7.8 points, with a high of 20 points. The older generation could still cut it.

Unlike the ABL, the WNBA had just a single-game playoff format. In the semi-finals, Houston defeated Charlotte 70–54, while the Liberty took an easy 59–41 victory over Phoenix. That meant the league's two best teams, Houston and New York, would meet in a single game for the championship. The game was played at the Summit Arena in Houston, where 16,285 fans came out to watch.

The game was close for the first half. Houston had a narrow 28–24 lead. But in the second half, the Liberty began missing shots and Cynthia Cooper put on a spectacular offensive display, justifying her selection as the league's MVP. Cooper wound up with 25 points, and the Comets wound up the first WNBA champions, with a 65–51 victory. In addition to her scoring, Cooper also had 4 rebounds, 4 assists, and 2 steals while playing the full 40 minutes. Tina Thompson, Houston's other All-League player, in just her first pro season out of USC, had 18 points and did a great defensive job on Rebecca Lobo, who finished with just 9. So it was the veteran and the rookie who led the way.

"I'll tell you when we won this thing," Coach Chancellor said. "We were in Cleveland earlier this season, and I called both [Cooper and Thompson] into my room. I said, 'One of you has to be Michael Jordan and the other has to be Scottie Pippen.' And Tina said to me, 'I'll be Pippen.'"

In other words, the rookie would let the veteran show the way. Thompson would lend all the support she could. And that's how it happened.

Cooper had performed like a player on a mission. And, in a sense, she was. She was playing not only for herself and her team but for her mother, Mary Cobbs, as well. Cobbs had been diagnosed with breast cancer in March. Not only was Cynthia Cooper playing at an MVP level, she was helping to care for her three younger sisters while giving her mother moral support, all at the same time.

"I dedicate this game to my mom," she said afterward. "She's *my* MVP."

It was a fitting end to a successful first season, one that saw the league average nearly

10,000 fans a game. Phoenix had the best attendance, averaging 13,703 fans, followed closely by the Liberty with 13,207. League president Val Ackerman couldn't have been happier.

"We'd hoped to attract a fan base that included families, women, and the core basketball fan who might be in withdrawal after the end of the NBA season," she said. "We guessed right about whom we'd attract, but we underestimated their number. And we didn't expect the intensity of the attraction."

Where to Now?

The Women's National Basketball Association certainly had a successful first season—at the gate, on the court, and in the marketing arenas. The league signed 14 corporate sponsors to three-year contracts and has a strong television commitment. McDonald's became the first sponsor to produce commercials featuring WNBA and NBA players together. Kellogg's launched a limited edition of its Special K cereal box featuring the winners of the WNBA championship.

Sears, the nation's largest department store, committed $10 million to an advertising campaign for its WNBA merchandise. The campaign includes TV spots and local contests at children's basketball programs. And General Motors donated more than $500,000—50 cents for every fan attending a WNBA game—to breast cancer research. The league was firing on all cylinders.

The WNBA will continue to market its big stars. They will also add two new teams, located in Detroit and Washington, D.C., in 1998. Shortly after the first season ended, the league got a big boost when Nikki McCray, the ABL's Most Valuable Player, crossed over to the WNBA, citing the greater marketing opportunities and exposure available through the WNBA. But she was the only one.

Yet there are those who still say the ABL has more top players. Though still operating on a smaller budget, the ABL isn't about to go away. It began its second season in October 1997. The league has expanded, adding the Long Beach (California) StingRays. Olympic star Katrina McClain returned from Europe to be reunited with Teresa Edwards on the Atlanta Glory. Edwards is also the league's first player/coach.

That isn't all. The ABL also added former Boston Celtics star and later coach K. C. Jones, as coach of the New England Blizzard. Jones's résumé includes 12 NBA titles as a player and coach. The Richmond Rage were moved to Philadelphia, where Dawn Staley & Company can do their thing in a huge basketball town. College stars Kara Wolters (New England) and Kate Starbird (Seattle) will be performing in the same regions as their collegiate triumphs.

The ABL has also picked up a television contract with Fox Sports to carry 16 regular-season games, the All-Star Game, and up to seven playoff games. Black Entertainment Television will air 12 games. Both Nike and Reebok will have print ad campaigns for the league. With all that activity, maybe the two leagues can not only coexist but prosper at the same time.

"The WNBA is just helping us as far as exposure," said ABL All-Star Debbie Black of the Colorado Xplosion. "People are asking their own states, 'Do we have a women's basketball team?'"

There is little doubt now that professional basketball for women is a sport whose time has come. "We got next!" and "Little girls need big girls to look up to!" have both proved excellent maxims containing a basketful of truths. Ultimately, it will be the fans who decide the fate of the sport in the United States. Women from every generation seem to take a special pride in the two pro leagues. The little girls truly do have big girls to look up to. Older women wish they had when they were young.

One 31-year-old New Yorker had never gone to a basketball game before the Liberty came along.

"We're seeing role models that we've never seen in other sports," she said. "I grew up idolizing Chris Evert-Lloyd [the all-time tennis great] and played organized tennis. Had the WNBA been around 20 years ago, I probably would have played basketball."

And another new fan, a grandmother from Phoenix, had never followed pro sports in her life. But once the Phoenix Mercury came along, she never missed a single game. But it was her reasoning that really spoke volumes for many fans of women's pro basketball.

"Everything has always been about men," she said. "Now it's about women, and it's wonderful."